The Naming of Black Beauty
and other horse stories

Compiled by Vic Parker

Miles Kelly

First published in 2014 by Miles Kelly Publishing Ltd
Harding's Barn, Bardfield End Green, Thaxted, Essex, CM6 3PX, UK

2 4 6 8 10 9 7 5 3

Publishing Director Belinda Gallagher
Creative Director Jo Cowan
Editorial Director Rosie Neave
Senior Editor Claire Philip
Designer Rob Hale
Production Elizabeth Collins, Caroline Kelly
Reprographics Stephan Davis, Jennifer Cozens, Thom Allaway
Assets Lorraine King

ISBN 978-1-78209-456-2

Printed in China

British Library Cataloguing-in-Publication Data
A catalogue record for this book is available from the British Library

ACKNOWLEDGEMENTS
The publishers would like to thank the following artists who have contributed to this book:
Advocate Art: Simon Mendez (Cover)
The Bright Agency: Mélanie Florian, Kirsteen Harris-Jones (inc. borders)

Made with paper from a sustainable forest

www.mileskelly.net
info@mileskelly.net

Contents

Old Gunpowder and the Ghost

From *The Legend of Sleepy Hollow* by Washington Irving

*This story is set over 200 years ago in North America.
At the beginning, a schoolteacher called Ichabod Crane arrives
in an area of quiet countryside inhabited by Dutch settlers.
He hopes to win the hand of Katrina Van Tassel, a wealthy
farmer's daughter, but so does another man, Brom Bones.*

ICHABOD SPENT AT LEAST an extra half
hour getting ready, dusting off his one and
only suit, and arranging his locks by a bit of
broken looking-glass that hung up in the
schoolhouse. He borrowed a horse from a

neighbouring farmer and set out like a gallant knight in quest of adventures.

In reality, the animal he rode was an old and tired plough-horse. It was bony, with a drooping neck, and a head like a hammer. The horse had a rusty mane and its tail was tangled and knotted. One eye had clouded over and was glassy and glaring, while the other had a mischievous gleam in it. In his day he must have had fire and courage, because his name was Gunpowder.

Ichabod was a suitable rider for such a steed. He rode with short stirrups, which brought his knees nearly up to the pommel of the saddle, and his sharp elbows stuck out like grasshoppers' knees. He carried his whip straight up in his hand, like a sceptre, and, as his horse jogged on, his arms flapped like a pair of wings.

It was a fine autumnal day. Ichabod and Gunpowder journeyed along the side of a range of hills that looked out upon the mighty Hudson river. The sun gradually dipped down in the west and it was towards evening that he arrived at the mansion of the Van Tassel family.

It was thronged with country folk and soon Ichabod found himself enjoying the charms of a genuine Dutch country tea-table, heaped up with delicious food.

Then came the dancing, and Ichabod was overjoyed that Katrina Van Tassel agreed to be his partner. On the other hand, Brom Bones, sorely smitten with love and jealousy, sat brooding by himself in one corner, watching with a beady eye.

Later, Ichabod spoke to some older folks, who sat with Katrina's father, discussing old times and drawing out long stories about the war. Each storyteller dressed up his tale with a few extra details, but all these war adventures were nothing to the ghost stories

that soon followed. The neighbourhood was rich in such spooky tales, largely due to the closeness of a glade called Sleepy Hollow. Rumour said it was haunted. Many tales were told about a great tree where mourning cries and wailings were heard.

Most of the stories centred upon the favourite ghost of Sleepy Hollow, the Headless Horseman, who had been heard lately near an old churchyard.

Eventually the revel gradually broke up and the partygoers began to make their way home. Ichabod lingered to have a private talk with Katrina, fully convinced that he was now on the road to winning her hand. What they spoke about I do not know. However, it clearly did not go as well as he had hoped, for he left after a short time, looking rather upset. He went straight to the stable and woke old Gunpowder from the comfortable quarters in which he was sleeping, dreaming of corn and oats.

It was the very witching time of night when Ichabod, heavy-hearted, pursued his travels homewards, along the sides of the lofty hills, which he had passed so cheerily in the afternoon. There were no signs of life except the melancholy chirp of a cricket, or the twang of a bullfrog.

The night grew darker and darker, the stars seemed to sink deeper in the sky, and driving clouds occasionally hid them from his sight. All the ghost stories he had heard now came crowding upon his thoughts.

His heart began to thump as he approached Sleepy Hollow and neared a bridge over a stream. Suddenly, something dark and towering rose up in the gloom at his side, like a gigantic monster.

With a scramble and a bound, it stood at once in the middle of the road, very close to Gunpowder and Ichabod. In the darkness, Ichabod could make out what looked like a huge rider, mounted on a powerful horse.

He pressed Gunpowder forward in the hope of escape, but the dark horseman and his steed kept pace with every step.

Then, suddenly the clouds parted and the moon shone down. To Ichabod's horror, he saw that the horseman was headless! And the head that should have rested on his

shoulders was actually being carried upon his saddle!

Ichabod's terror rose to desperation. He rained a shower of kicks upon Gunpowder and the horse dashed away, the ghostly horseman and his demon steed pelting after them. Gunpowder plunged headlong through Sleepy Hollow until Ichabod saw the walls of a church on the other side of the bridge. 'If I can only reach that,' he thought, 'I am safe.'

The steed was panting and blowing

close behind him, and even fancied that he felt his hot breath. Another kick in the ribs, and old Gunpowder galloped into the churchyard. Ichabod cast a look behind to see if his pursuer would vanish in a flash of fire on reaching holy ground. But he saw the horseman rise in his stirrups and hurl his head at him! Ichabod tried to dodge it, but it hit his own head. With a tremendous crash he tumbled into the dust.

Next morning old Gunpowder was found without his saddle, and with his bridle under his feet, cropping the grass at the gate of the farmer who owned him. And at the churchyard entrance there lay a smashed pumpkin. But there was no sign of Ichabod…

Pegasus, the Winged Horse

By James Baldwin

Pegasus is one of the most famous horses of all time. According to the myths of ancient Greece, he was a son of the god of the ocean, Poseidon. There are many stories about the partnership between Pegasus and a hero called Bellerophon.

PEOPLE SAID THAT THE GODS sent him to the earth. But to this day nobody really knows anything about how Pegasus came to exist.

One day, full of energy and strength, he

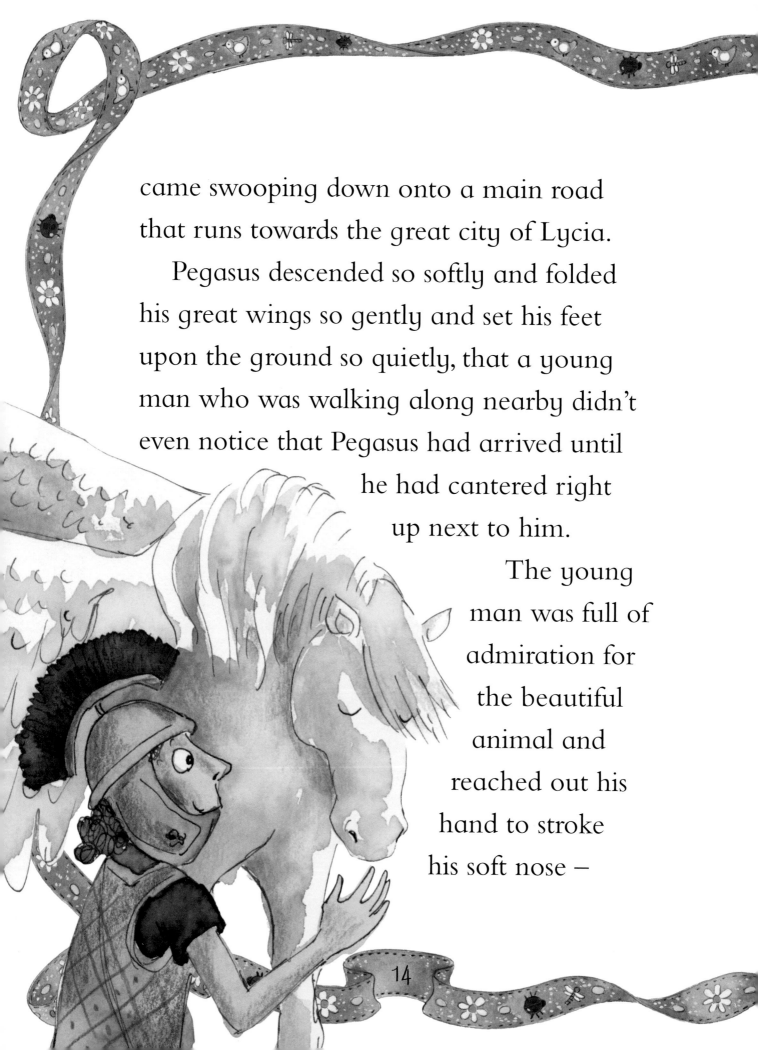

came swooping down onto a main road that runs towards the great city of Lycia.

Pegasus descended so softly and folded his great wings so gently and set his feet upon the ground so quietly, that a young man who was walking along nearby didn't even notice that Pegasus had arrived until he had cantered right up next to him.

The young man was full of admiration for the beautiful animal and reached out his hand to stroke his soft nose –

14

the horse turned away and flew off as quick as an arrow.

The young man walked on, but the horse returned and gambolled playfully around him, sometimes trotting back and forth, sometimes rising in the air and sailing in circles round and round him. At last, the young man coaxed the horse close enough to leap onto his back.

By late in the afternoon, when they had left the pleasant farmland around Lycia far behind them, they landed at the border of a wild, deserted region. An old man with a long white beard and bright glittering eyes met them and stopped to admire the beautiful animal.

"Who are you, young man," he inquired,

"and what are you doing with so handsome a steed here in this lonely place?"

"My name is Bellerophon," answered the young man, "and I am going by order of King Lobates to the country beyond the northern mountains, where I am going to try to slay a fire-breathing monster called the Chimaera, which lives there. I cannot tell you where this horse comes from or who he belongs to, for I do not know."

The old man was silent for a few moments, then said, "Do you see the white roof over there among the trees? Under it there is a shrine to the goddess Athena, of which I am the keeper. A few steps beyond it is my own humble cottage. If you will go in and lodge with me for the night, I may

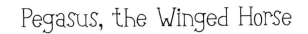

be able to tell you something about the task that you have undertaken."

Bellerophon was very glad to accept the old man's invitation, for the sun had already begun to dip below the western hills. The hut was small but clean and cosy. The kind host gave Bellerophon supper, made him comfortable, and then looked him straight in the eye and said, "Now tell me all about yourself and why you are going alone into the country of the Chimaera."

"My father," answered Bellerophon, "is King Glaucus of Corinth. I am brave and fond of hunting wild beasts, and am anxious to win fame by doing some daring deed. I heard that the people who live on the other side of the northern mountains are in great dread of a strange animal called the Chimaera that comes out of the caves and carries off their flocks, and sometimes their children too. I made up my mind to kill it. So I found the shortest road to the mountains and – here I am!"

Then the old man said, "I have heard of this Chimaera and know that no man has ever fought with that monster and lived. For it is a more terrible beast than you would believe. The head and shoulders are those of a lion, the body is that of a goat, and the back parts are those of a dragon. It fights with hot breath and a long tail. At night it stays on the mountains, then by day it goes down into the valleys. All the region beyond the mountains has been laid waste by the

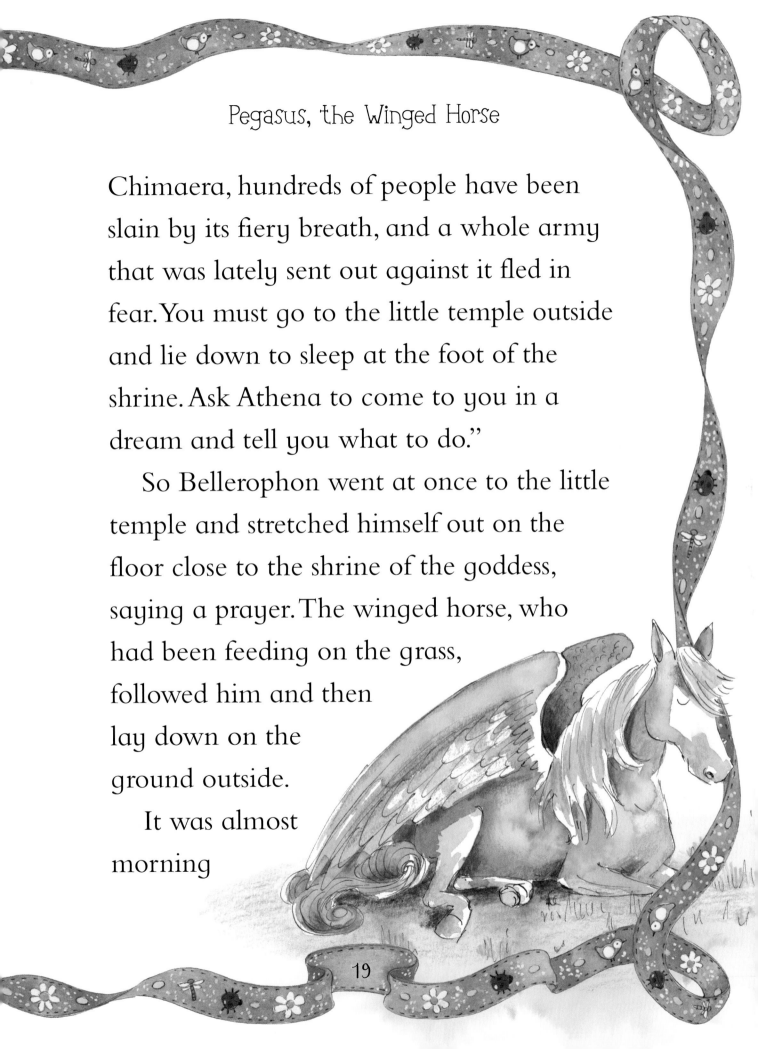

Chimaera, hundreds of people have been slain by its fiery breath, and a whole army that was lately sent out against it fled in fear. You must go to the little temple outside and lie down to sleep at the foot of the shrine. Ask Athena to come to you in a dream and tell you what to do."

So Bellerophon went at once to the little temple and stretched himself out on the floor close to the shrine of the goddess, saying a prayer. The winged horse, who had been feeding on the grass, followed him and then lay down on the ground outside.

It was almost morning

when Bellerophon dreamed that a tall and stately lady came into the temple and stood beside him.

"Do you know who the winged steed is that waits outside for you?" she asked.

"I do not," answered Bellerophon. "But if I had some means of making him understand me, he might be my helper."

"His name is Pegasus," said the lady, "and he was born near the shore of the great western ocean. He has come to help you fight the Chimaera. You can guide him anywhere if you put this ribbon into his mouth and hold on tightly to the ends."

With these words, she placed a beautiful bridle in Bellerophon's hands, and then walked silently away.

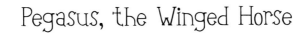

When the sun had risen and Bellerophon awoke, the bridle was lying on the floor beside him, and near it was a long bow with arrows and a shield. It was the first bridle that he had ever seen — indeed, some people believe it was the first ever bridle to be made. The young man went out and quickly slipped the ribbon bit into the mouth of Pegasus, and leaped upon his back. To his great joy, Bellerophon saw that now the horse understood all of his wishes.

"Here are your bow and arrows and your shield," cried the old man, handing them to him. "May Athena be with you in your fight against the Chimaera!"

At a word from Bellerophon, Pegasus rose high in the air and then headed towards the great mountains.

It was evening when they arrived. Bellerophon saw the Chimaera crouching in the shadow of a cliff. He fitted an arrow in his bow and shot it directly at its head.

The arrow missed the mark and struck the beast in the throat. You should have seen the fury of the Chimaera! It reared up and blew its fiery breath towards Pegasus.

"Pegasus," Bellerophon cried, "steady yourself so I can send her another gift!"

This time the arrow struck the beast in the back. It attacked everything in its reach and filled all the mountain-valleys with the noise of mad roaring. Bellerophon's third arrow pierced the horrid creature to the heart. The Chimaera fell backwards lifeless,

and rolled down the steep mountainside.

Bellerophon found the Chimaera lying stiff and dead the next morning. He cut off the creature's head, and was about to head home when he had an idea – why shouldn't he ride on the back of Pegasus all the way to the gates of heaven?

He would have surely got there if the great god Zeus hadn't noticed him just as he was about to enter. Angered by Bellerophon's boldness, Zeus sent a gadfly to sting the horse. Pegasus made a wild plunge to escape the fly, and Bellerophon, taken by surprise, tumbled back down to the earth.

Luckily the hero was not killed by this fall, but he was blinded. Pegasus flew off, never to be heard of or seen again.

The Naming of Black Beauty

From *Black Beauty* by Anna Sewell

In this extract from Black Beauty *the young horse is taken away from the farm on which he was born. Bought by the wealthiest man in a local village, Squire Gordon, he settles quite happily into life on his country estate and is given a name at last…*

I **LIVED FOR SOME YEARS** with Squire Gordon. Squire Gordon's park skirted the village of Birtwick. It was entered by a large iron gate, at which stood the first lodge, and then you trotted along on a smooth road between clumps of large old trees, then there was another lodge and another gate, which brought you to the house and the gardens. Beyond this lay the paddock, the old orchard and the stables.

There was stabling for many horses and carriages. I was taken into a very roomy one, with four good stalls. A large swinging window opened into the yard, which made it pleasant and airy. The first stall was a large square one, shut behind with a wooden gate. The others were common stalls, good stalls, but not nearly so large.

Mine had a low rack for hay and a low manger for corn. It was called a loose box, because the horse that was put into it was not tied up, but left loose, to do as he liked.

The sides were low enough so that I

could see all that went on through the iron rails that were at the top. The groom gave me some very nice oats, he patted me, spoke kindly, and then went away.

When I had eaten my corn I looked round. In the stall next to mine stood a little fat grey pony, with a thick mane and tail, a

very pretty head, and a pert little nose.

I put my head up to the iron rails at the top of my box, and said, "How do you do? What is your name?"

He held up his head, and said, "My name is Merrylegs. I am very handsome, I carry the young ladies on my back, and sometimes I take our mistress out in the carriage. They think a great deal of me. So, are you going to live next door to me in the box?"

I said, "Yes."

"Well, then," he said, "I hope you are good-tempered, I do not like anyone next door who bites."

Just then a horse's head looked over from the stall beyond, the ears were laid back, and the eye looked rather ill-tempered. This was a tall chestnut mare, with a long handsome neck. She looked across to me and said, "So it is you who has turned me out of my box, it is a very strange thing for a colt like you to come and turn a lady out of her own home."

"I beg your pardon," I said, "I have turned no one out, the man who brought me put me here, and I had nothing to do with it, and as to my being a colt, I am turned four years old and am a grown-up horse. I never had words yet with horse or mare and it is my wish to live in peace."

"Well," she said, "we shall see."

I said no more.

In the afternoon, when she went out,

Merrylegs told me about her.

"The thing is this," said Merrylegs. "Ginger has a bad habit of biting and snapping – that is why they call her Ginger,

and when she was in the loose box she used to snap very much. One day she bit the groom's boy, James, in the arm and made it bleed, and so Miss Flora and Miss Jessie, who are very fond of me, were afraid to come into the stable. They used to bring me nice things to eat, an apple or a carrot, or a piece of bread, but after Ginger stood in that box they dared not come, and I missed them very much indeed. I hope they will now come again, if you do not bite or snap."

I told him I never bit anything but grass, hay, and corn, and could not think what pleasure Ginger found in it.

"Well, I don't think she does find pleasure," says Merrylegs, "it is just a bad habit, she says no one was ever kind to her, and why should she not bite? Of course, it is a very bad habit, but I am sure, if all she says be true, she must have been very ill-used before she came here. John does all he can to please her, and James does all he can, and our master never uses a whip if a horse acts right, so I think she might be good-tempered here.

"You see," he said, with a wise look, "I am twelve years old, I know a great deal, and I can tell you there is not a better place for a horse all round the country than this. John is the best groom that ever was - he has been here fourteen years, and you never saw such a kind boy as James is, so it is all Ginger's own fault."

The next day I was prepared for my master to ride. I remembered my mother's advice and I tried to do exactly what he wanted me to do.

I found that he was a very good rider

and thoughtful for his horse too.

When he came home, Mrs Gordon was at the hall door as he rode up.

"Well, my dear," she said, "how do you like him?"

"He is exactly what John said," he replied, "a pleasanter creature I never wish to mount. What shall we call him?"

"What about Ebony?" said she, "For he is as black as ebony."

Squire Gordon thought for a moment, then declared, "No, not Ebony."

"What about Blackbird, like your uncle's old horse?"

"No, he is far more handsome than old Blackbird ever was."

"Well," she said, "he is really quite a

beauty, and he has such a sweet face – what do you say to calling him Black Beauty?"

"Black Beauty… Why, yes, I think that is a very good name. If you like, it shall be his name," decided Squire Gordon.

And so it was.

The War Horse of Alexander

By Andrew Lang

Alexander the Great was a powerful military leader who lived over two thousand years ago. He led invading armies over Europe and into Asia to create one of the largest ever empires. His horse, Bucephalus, is almost as legendary, and has been described as a massive, black creature with a white star upon his enormous brow.

THERE ARE NOT NEARLY AS MANY stories about horses as there are about dogs and cats, yet almost every great general has had his favourite horse, who has gone with him through many campaigns and borne him safely in many battlefields.

The most famous horse who ever lived was perhaps one belonging to the ancient Macedonian king, Alexander the Great. His noble horse was called Bucephalus. This is how Alexander came by him…

When Alexander was just a boy, a trader presented Bucephalus to his father, King Philip of Macedon. The trader offered him for the very large sum of thirteen talents, which was the type of money used in Macedon. Beautiful though the horse looked, the king wisely refused to buy him before knowing what his character was like.

So King Philip ordered Bucephalus to be led into a neighbouring field and asked a groom to mount him. But it soon became apparent that the horse wouldn't let anyone come near him – when even the best and most experienced riders approached him, he reared up on his hind legs, and they were forced to back away.

The trader was told to take his horse away, for the king would have none of him. However the king's son, Alexander, stood by watching all that went on, and his heart went out to the beautiful creature.

He cried out to his father, "Stop! We are going to lose a good horse because no one has the skill to mount him!"

King Philip heard these words and agreed it was a terrible shame to let the horse be taken away. He thought to himself for a moment, then turned to his son and said, "Do you think that you, who are young and haven't been riding long, can ride this horse better than older, expert riders?"

To which Alexander answered, "I know I can ride this horse better than any of them. Please let me try."

"But if you fail," said King Philip, "I will have lost a huge amount of money in paying for him!"

Alexander laughed out loud and said with glee, "I will give you the money then." And so it was settled.

So Alexander drew near to the horse and took him by the bridle, turning his face to the sun so that he might not be frightened by the movements of his own shadow, for the prince had noticed that it scared him greatly.

Then Alexander stroked the horse's head and led him forwards. The second the horse began to get uneasy, the prince suddenly leaped onto his back and took charge of him with firm hands upon the bridle.

As soon as Bucephalus gave up trying to throw his rider, and only pawed the ground Alexander shook the reins and, bidding him go, they flew away like lightning. Taming Bucephalus was Alexander's first conquest. His father said, "Macedonia is obviously too small a country for you – you should go out and conquer other challenges."

So from that moment on, Bucephalus made it clear that he served Alexander alone – he wouldn't let anyone else ride him.

Bucephalus bore Alexander through all his battles and even when wounded, as he once was at the taking of Thebes, would not suffer his master to mount another horse. Together they swam rivers, crossed mountains, conquered kingdoms and won lands.

When, after ten years of adventures and victories, old Bucephalus died, Alexander was heartbroken. He gave his horse the most splendid funeral he could think of, with a grand tomb. And around it, so his memory would never die, he built a magnificent city and called it Bucephalia.